Bobby
and the
Great, Green
Booger

Bobby
and the
Great, Green
Booger

written by
Debbie Dadey

illustrated by
Mike Gordon

For my favorite carpool boogers:
Halley Baker, Becky Dadey, and Lindsey Stoltz

Second printing by Willowisp Press 1997.

Published by Willowisp Press
801 94th Avenue North, St. Petersburg, Florida 33702

Printed in the United States of America

2   4   6   8   10   9   7   5   3

I S B N   0 - 8 7 4 0 6 - 8 4 5 - 2

Table of Contents

Chapter 1
Furball

My name is Bobby Carson and I
hate to sneeze. I really hate to, but
I do it a lot. I don't mean to—it just
happens. Lots of things make me,
like dust and chalk.

My best friend Andrew's cat makes me sneeze a lot. I hug it even though it makes me sneeze.

"You shouldn't hug Furball," Andrew told me.

I nodded my head and squeezed Furball one more time. "I know." I liked Furball and Furball liked me.

So I hugged him again.

I sneezed.

Furball purred.

"We'd better get to school,"
Andrew told me.

I hugged Furball one more time
and picked up my backpack.
Andrew and I started walking to
school. Furball stayed at Andrew's
house.

On the way to school, we met
Pat pulling a wagon. The wagon had
a big cardboard box in it. "Hi, Pat!"
Andrew said.

"What's in the wagon?" I asked,
sneezing again.

Pat smiled, showing an empty
space where his top teeth used to be.
"It's a secret surprise!"

Chapter 2
Secret Surprise

"A secret?" Andrew's eyes got big.

"A surprise?!" I said. My eyes were full of water. They did that when I sneezed a lot.

"If you promise not to tell, I'll let you see. It's for Show-and-Tell," Pat told us.

I nodded my head and sneezed.
Andrew just nodded his head.

Pat opened the top to the box
just a little. Andrew and I peeked
inside.

"Wow!" Andrew said.

"Wow!" I said.

"Kittens," Pat said, smiling again. "My mom is going to come get them at snack time. I can see if anyone wants one."

There were five tiny kittens in the box. Two were gray and three were white.

I picked up a small white kitten. I hugged it. Now my eyes were big and watery. "You mean to *have?*" I asked.

Pat nodded his head. "My mom said I can't keep all of them. She said I can give them away to good homes."

"I have a good home," I told Pat.

"You also are allergic to cats," Andrew reminded me.

Ach-choo! I sneezed again and nodded my head sadly. My mom wouldn't want me to sneeze all the time. She wouldn't want a cat, even if we do have a good home. I put the white kitten back into the box.

"We'd better get to school before the bell rings," I told Pat.

Andrew and I walked behind the wagon. Pat walked in front of the wagon because he was pulling it. We made it to school right before the bell rang.

I sat at my desk and sneezed. My nose felt funny so I sniffed. Then the bell rang. My second grade teacher stood at the front of the room and smiled at us. All of us sat down in our seats. We got quiet. Miss Allen kept smiling.

"Guess what?" Miss Allen asked the class.

We all shrugged and squirmed in our seats. Something was different. Usually Miss Allen started the day with the Pledge. She never started the day by asking, "Guess what?" Maybe our class had won a prize—maybe a zillion dollars!

Chapter 3
Good News

"I have good news," Miss Allen told us. "We get to be the first class to use the brand-new math computer lab!"

"Yes!" Everyone cheered and clapped. It wasn't quite as great as winning a zillion dollars, but it was pretty good news.

Miss Allen held up her hand for us to stop clapping. "I have some other news," she said.

Uh, oh. I didn't like the way Miss Allen said that. I hoped it wasn't bad news. It was.

"We need to practice our math facts all morning to get ready to use the lab," Miss Allen said.

"Oh," groaned the class. I like math. I like math a lot. But I don't like to practice anything too much.

First, we said the Pledge and
collected the lunch money. Then
Miss Allen had a bunch of us go
to the board to try math problems.
We did the problems like a race.
I usually got the right answer,
but I wasn't very fast.

"Fourteen minus six," said Miss Allen.

I wrote the problem:

$14 - 6 = 8$.

I was right. I erased the problem.

"Very good," said Miss Allen.
"Ten plus nine."

I wrote the problem:
10+9=19.

I was right. I erased the
problem. The chalk dust made me
sneeze. I wiped my nose on my
sleeve.

"Try this one," said Miss Allen.
"Seven plus five."
I wrote:
7+5=

Then I sneezed. I sneezed again.
I wrote the answer 12 and
sneezed again. Chalk dust usually
makes me sneeze, but not that
much. I sneezed again and my
eyes got watery.

I looked down. Right by my feet was the box that Pat had brought to school. Inside were the kittens. I could hear them purring. The kittens and the chalk dust were working together to make me sneeze.

They were doing a good job. I was sneezing a lot. I couldn't even hear what Miss Allen was saying.

That's when it happened. It was something very bad.

MEOW

Chapter 4
Terrible

It was something terrible. It was my biggest sneeze ever. It was the biggest sneeze ever in the history of the world.

But the sneeze wasn't so bad. It was what it made.

It made a
booger. Not a little
booger—it made a big
booger. The sneeze made
a great, green booger.

I didn't know it at first. But I did know that everyone was laughing. Everyone laughed at me. Actually, they were laughing at my booger. Miss Allen even had her hand over her mouth. She was trying not to laugh.

First, I got mad. Then I got madder. I was so mad I felt like crying. "Don't laugh at me!" I yelled.

Then Andrew patted my shoulder. "Bobby, you do look funny with a big booger hanging out of your nose. Look." He handed me a mirror from the science corner.

I looked in the mirror. I looked at my booger. It was big. It was green. It was a great, green booger. It was funny-looking.

I smiled. I smiled at my booger. Then I laughed. "Maybe I'll save it," I told the class.

Miss Allen gave me a small box. I put my booger in it.

"Bobby, you are a good sport," Miss Allen said. "Go to the bathroom and wipe your nose and wash your hands. We'll have a surprise for you when you get back."

"We'll have a secret surprise," said Pat.

Chapter 5
Science

When I came back from the
bathroom, everyone smiled at me.
The boys and girls pointed to the
science corner. There was my
booger in Miss Allen's box.

There was a big sign beside it.
The sign said: *The Great Green
Booger by Bobby Carson*

I smiled. "We can study it with our microscope," I told Miss Allen.

Miss Allen nodded and pointed to the sign again. "Look what Pat wrote in small letters."

I looked at the sign again. Under my name it said: *Made from hugging kittens and being allergic.*

The whole class laughed. I did, too. Then Pat showed his kittens to the class. A lot of kids wanted to take one home.

Pat's mother came. We ate our snacks and Pat's mother wrote down some names. She would call their parents. She didn't write down my name.

I stopped sneezing after Pat's mom left. The kittens left with her. It was good not to sneeze anymore. I looked at the science corner. I looked at the box with my booger and the sign. I was glad the kittens had left.

I didn't want to make
another great, green
booger—at least not today.

About the Author

Debbie Dadey is a former teacher and librarian. She loves being a full-time writer and visiting schools.

She lives in Aurora, Illinois, with her husband Eric. They have two children, Nathan and Rebekah. The family also has a puppy named Bailey.

Bobby and the Great, Green Booger is Debbie Dadey's forty-seventh book for young readers.

About the Artist

Mike Gordon moved from England to California, where he now lives with his two children, Kim and Jay.

He draws all day to keep up with the many books that are wanted. Fortunately there is an endless supply of ideas from his children and their friends! Mike has completed illustrations for more than 100 books, as well as hundreds of greeting cards.

His hobbies are learning piano and eating chocolate chip ice cream.